DIGGERSAURS EXPLORE

Michael Whaite

Random House New York

When work is done, it's time for FUN!
DIGGERSAURS
are ROARING.

"We might find GOLD
or something OLD!
We love to go EXPLORING!"

First they see . . .

a FALLEN TREE.

STRETCH!

Oooh...
my knees!

That stops them in their tracks.

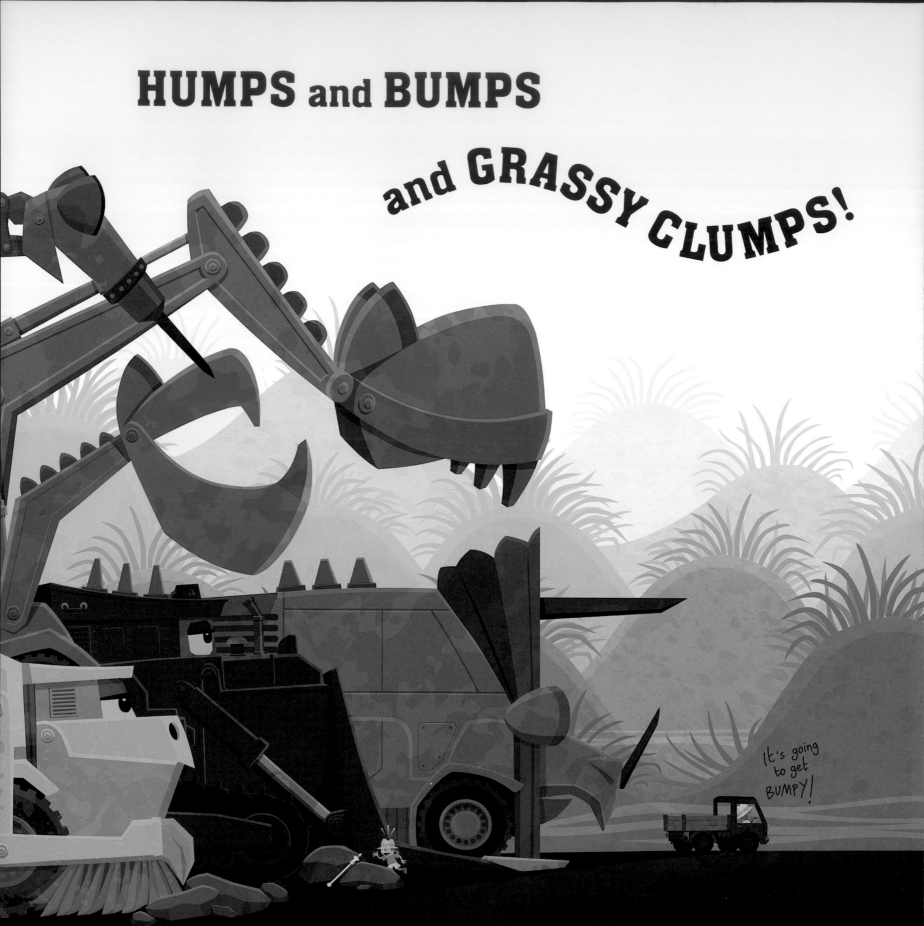

HUMPS and BUMPS

and GRASSY CLUMPS!

It's going to get BUMPY!

"You **ROLL**, I'll **MOW**—and off we go!"

But then a **WALL**
so wide and tall!

It looks like they're in trouble.

What's this? **A SLOPE!**
They'll need a rope—

it's far too steep to climb!

Goin' underground!

At last they reach
a sandy beach.
Suddenly,
a sound . . .

What's that BUZZ?

What's this?

"My tail . . . because
there's metal underground!"

"Come on—let's **DIG!**
It's something **BIG!**"

CHOMP!!

"It's something washed ashore."

And he roars, "Thanks, **DIGGERSAURS**. I've been stuck here for years!

I've missed the sea, but now I'm free! Please help me shift my gears."

DIGGERSAURS PUSH!
With one big WHOOOSH . . .

DIVERSAUR'S in motion.
A SPLASH! A ROAR!
He slides offshore . . .

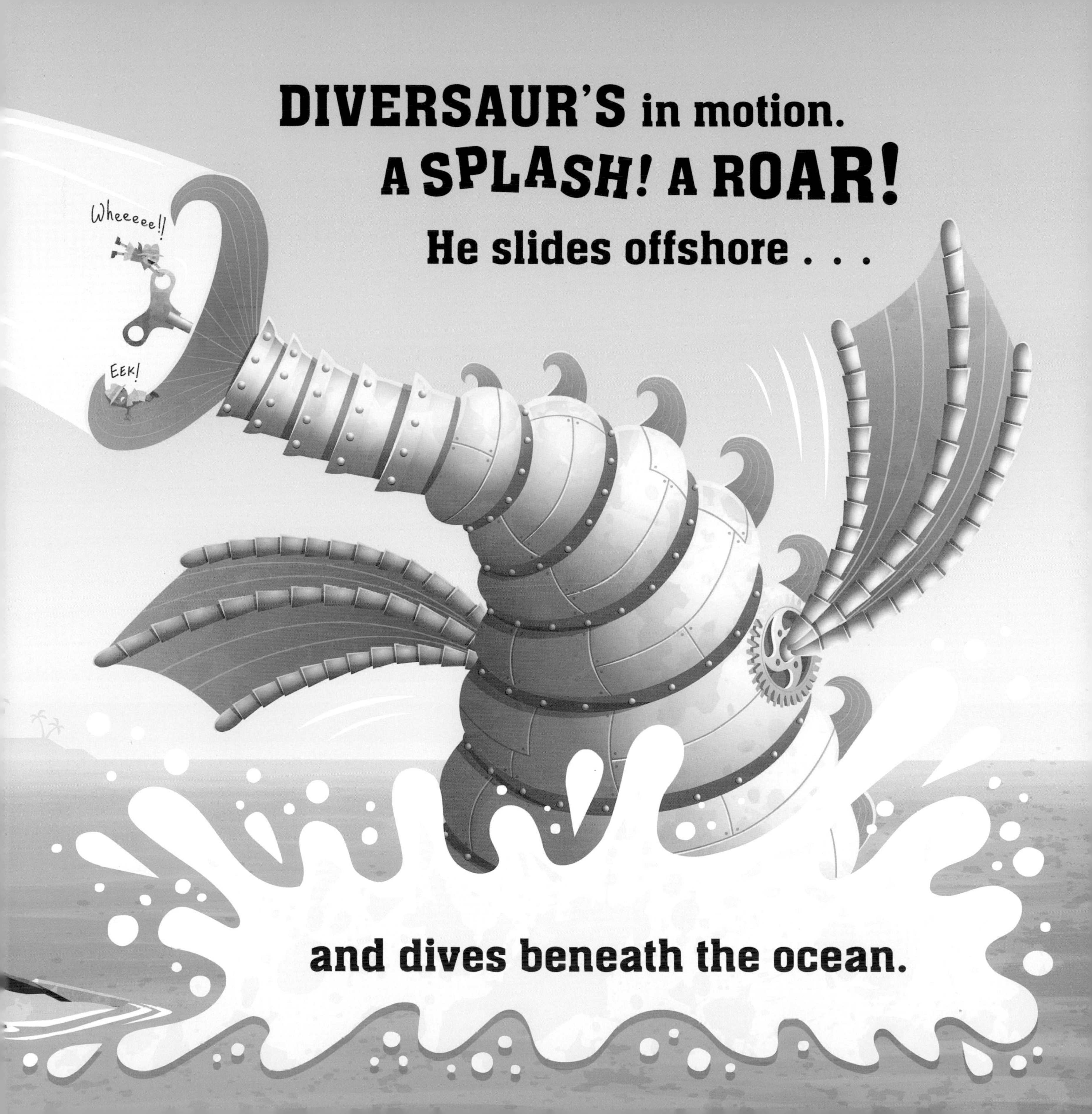

and dives beneath the ocean.

"We did find **GOLD**
and something **OLD**—

THE **GIANT** DIVERSAURUS!"

TREASURE!!!

And in the end
a newfound friend
for **DIGGERSAUR EXPLORERS!**